E E Pinkney, J. Brian.

Jojo's flying side
kick.

$15.00

		DATE	

BAKER & TAYLOR

JoJo's Flying Side Kick

Brian Pinkney

Simon & Schuster Books for Young Readers

A NOTE FROM THE AUTHOR

Tae Kwon Do is a martial art form that was created in ancient Korea. Tae means "to kick." Kwon means "to punch." And Do means "art." The translation of Tae Kwon Do is "the art of kicking and punching." Unlike Japanese karate, which translates to "the art of the open hand," Tae Kwon Do emphasizes kicking techniques over hand techniques.

Students of Tae Kwon Do wear a white uniform called a dobok, which is tied with a colored belt. The color of the belt represents the level of experience the student has achieved. Beginners wear white belts, then move on to yellow, green, blue, red, and finally black.

Today, Tae Kwon Do is studied by millions of people all over the world for exercise, self-defense, and as a way to gain self-confidence.

 Simon & Schuster Books for Young Readers
An imprint of Simon and Schuster Children's Publishing Division
1230 Avenue of the Americas
New York, NY 10020
Text and illustrations copyright © 1995 by Brian Pinkney

Simon & Schuster Books for Young Readers is a trademark of Simon & Schuster.

The text of this book is set in 14-point Hiroshige Medium.
The illustrations were done in scratchboard and oil.
Manufactured in the United States of America
10 9 8 7 6 5 4 3 2 1

Library of Congress Cataloging-in-Publication Data
Pinkney, J. Brian.
   JoJo's flying side kick / by Brian Pinkney.
      p.   cm.
   Summary: Everyone gives JoJo advice on how to perform in order to earn
her yellow belt in tae kwon do class, but in the end she figures it out for herself.
   ISBN 0-689-80283-8
   [1. Martial arts—Fiction.   2. Courage—Fiction.   3. Afro-Americans—Fiction.]   I. Title.
PZ7.P63347Jo   1995   [E]—dc20   94-24318

To Grand Master Kwon, Jae-Hwa

"To do a flying side kick," Master Kim explained, "jump like you can fly. Push out hard and fast with the heel of your foot and yell, 'KIAH!'"
Then he counted, "One! . . . Two! . . . Hah Na! . . . Dool! . . ." as JoJo and the other students practiced their flying side kicks at the Tae Kwon Do Center.

At the end of class, Master Kim spoke to JoJo. "You have been a very good white belt, JoJo. Now you're ready for the final test for your yellow belt promotion. To earn the yellow belt, you must break a board with a flying side kick. You'll be tested tomorrow."

"Yes, sir!" said JoJo.

Then she began to worry.

Grandaddy met JoJo after Tae Kwon Do class to walk her home. JoJo was glad because she hated to walk past the tree in her front yard. It looked like a creepy bandit.

"How's my little lady today?" Grandaddy asked. "Master Kim says you're going for your yellow belt promotion tomorrow. You must be nervous."

"I'm freakin' out," said JoJo.

"Well," said Grandaddy, "when I was young, and in my prime, butterflies fluttered in my stomach before every big boxing match."

Grandaddy moved his feet back and forth, and side to side. "Back in the day, I kept my hands up, stayed light on my toes, and did a little shuffle step to chase the jitters away."

JoJo copied Grandaddy's footwork and followed him around the driveway. "I like the way you move Grandaddy, but I don't see what dancing has to do with my promotion."

"You will," said Grandaddy.

As Grandaddy and JoJo turned to go into the house,
P.J. and Ted came up the street.
"Hey, JoJo!" P.J. yelled.
"Ah-Rooof!" barked Ted.

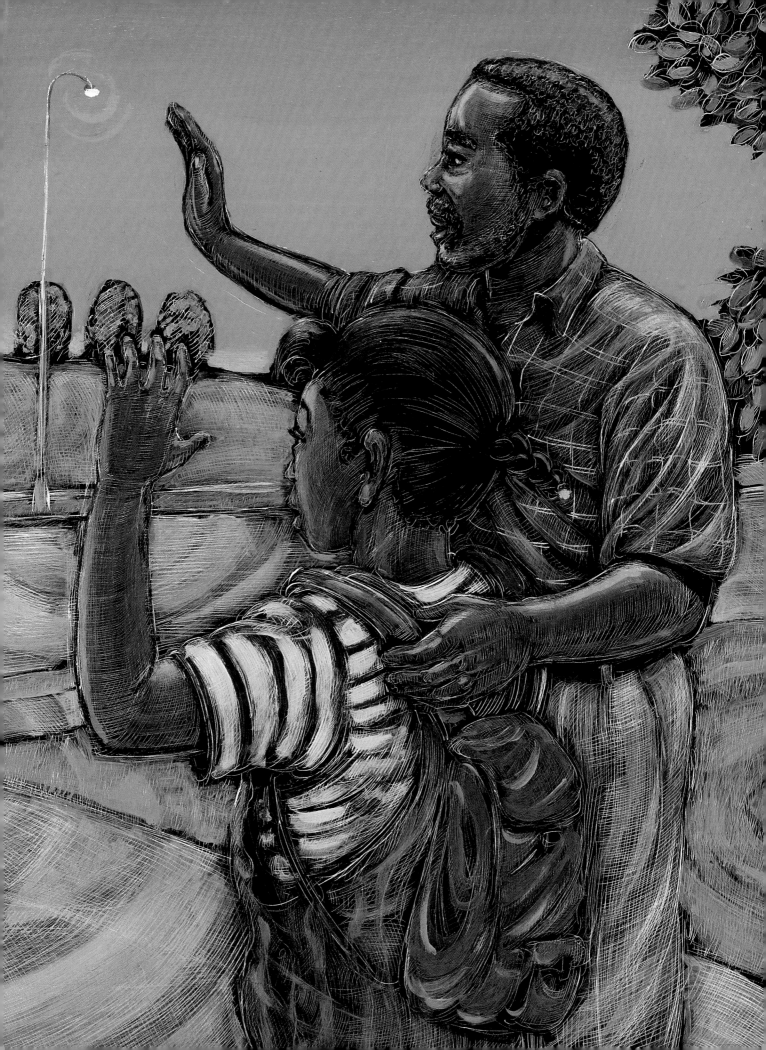

"I don't think you're strong enough to break a piece of wood tomorrow," P.J. said and jumped into the swing.

"Why not?" JoJo asked.

" 'Cause you yell like a mouse in class. When I do my kick, I yell 'KIAH' at the top of my lungs."

"So what?" JoJo took a step back from the tree.

"You'd get more power if the sound came from deep down in your stomach," P.J. explained. "Then, let your 'KIAH' come up and out of your mouth."

"Ah-ROOOF, ROOOF, ROOOF!" barked Ted.

"Hear that?" hollered P.J. "Even Ted does it!"

When P.J. and Ted walked off, JoJo froze. She was alone with the creepy tree bandit. She turned to go up the driveway, but the creepy tree bandit lunged at her when she tried to pass. JoJo ducked and ran into the house as fast as she could.

JoJo slammed the door.

"Hi, honey! Grandaddy says you're getting tested at Tae Kwon Do tomorrow," her mom said.

"I have to break a board with a flying side kick," JoJo said, "but what if I forget how to do it?"

"Why don't you visualize your technique?" JoJo's mom asked. "That's what I do before a tennis match."

"Visualize?" JoJo asked.

"Visualize. It's when you picture something in your mind," Mom explained. "Picture yourself doing the perfect flying side kick."

JoJo closed her eyes. But all she saw were dark shadows moving around in her head.

"Now, get a good night's sleep so you'll be ready for your big day tomorrow," Mom said.

But JoJo couldn't get to sleep. She lay awake, worrying about her promotion for her yellow belt. To add to JoJo's troubles, the creepy bandit tree moved back and forth outside her window. It even tried to climb in. JoJo closed her eyes and hid under the covers.

The next day in class, Master Kim called out, "Attention!"
Then he nodded to JoJo. "Begin!"
At the sound of Master Kim's voice, butterflies fluttered
in JoJo's stomach.

JoJo shuffled her feet back and forth, and side to side, the way Grandaddy had shown her. But, when she looked up at the piece of wood, she froze. In that moment, JoJo knew exactly what to do.

With all her might, JoJo leaped into the air. She focused on the piece of wood and visualized dark shadows and the creepy bandit tree.

From deep in her stomach, JoJo screamed . . .
"KEEYYAAHHH!"

And, with her perfect flying side kick, the board split
with a "CRAAACK!"

When JoJo landed, everyone applauded. Master Kim shook her hand. "Congratulations, JoJo!" he said, and he presented her with a bright new yellow belt.

That night, when they got home, Grandaddy said,
"I thought you didn't care for that swing, little lady."
    JoJo just smiled, threw back her head, and kicked up
to the sky.